2/83

7503

S0-BCL-978

The Boy
Who Wanted
A Family

HARPER & ROW, PUBLISHERS

NEW YORK

CAMBRIDGE   LONDON
HAGERSTOWN   MEXICO CITY
PHILADELPHIA   SÃO PAULO
SAN FRANCISCO *1817* SYDNEY

The Boy
Who Wanted
A Family

by Shirley Gordon

Pictures by Charles Robinson

To my son,
David Russell Gordon

The Boy Who Wanted a Family
Text copyright © 1980 by Shirley Gordon
Illustrations copyright © 1980 by Charles Robinson
Printed in
the United States of America. For information address
Harper & Row, Publishers, Inc., 10 East 53rd Street,
New York, N.Y. 10022. Published simultaneously in
Canada by Fitzhenry & Whiteside Limited, Toronto.
FIRST EDITION

Library of Congress Cataloging in Publication Data
Gordon, Shirley.
    The boy who wanted a family.

SUMMARY: Explores the hopes, fears, and experiences
of a young boy and his new mom during the one-year
waiting period before he can be legally adopted.
    [1. Adoption—Fiction]   I. Robinson, Charles,
1931–   II. Title.
PZ7.G6594Bo   [Fic]   79-2003
ISBN 0-06-022051-1
ISBN 0-06-022052-X lib. bdg.

Chapters

Birthday Wish   *1*

New Mom   *10*

Friends   *22*

Family   *34*

Superman   *45*

First Christmas   *53*

The Biggest Thing in the World   *65*

Special Day   *72*

A Visit to Court   *82*

Birthday Wish

Michael curled up into a ball under the covers and blinked back his tears again. He wasn't a crybaby, but the tears just came sometimes and he couldn't always stop them.

They weren't sad tears. They were *mad* tears.

Why wasn't I born lucky like other kids? He'd been asking himself that all his life. Why can't I have a *real* home, with a *real* mother and father? That wasn't a whole lot to ask, was it?

Instead, here he was—in another foster home. Michael didn't exactly know what "foster" meant, but he knew it didn't mean *real*. He liked his new foster "mom" and "dad," all right, but they weren't his real mother and father. He squirmed angrily in the bed, getting all twisted up in the covers.

In the dark room, he could hear the other kids breathing and snoring all around him. They were orphans—

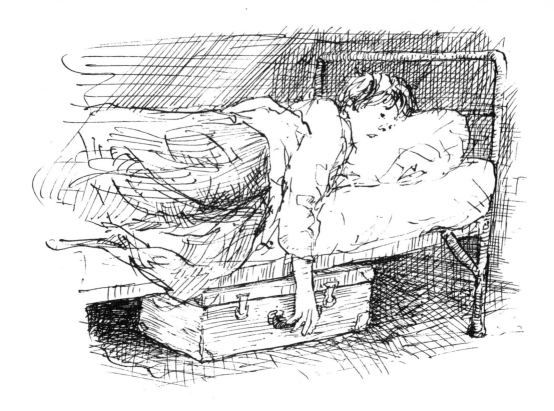

foster kids—too. At least he wasn't the only unlucky one
in the world.

He reached down under the bed to make sure his old
brown suitcase was still there. It's part of me, thought
Michael, rubbing his hand across the worn scratched
leather. It's been just about every place I've been.

There wasn't much in it, of course—his extra under-
wear and socks, some jeans and T-shirts, and a warm red
sweater that one of his foster brothers had outgrown.

2

(Michael couldn't even remember what that foster brother had looked like, he'd had so many in so many different homes.)

Stuffed in the corner of his suitcase, under his clothes, were Michael's favorite toys that he always took with him wherever he went—a miniature tow truck, its blue paint rusted from the time he forgot and left it out in the rain, and a deck of cards whose kings and queens had orange and purple crayon marks all over their faces.

The foster mother he had then had spanked him because she said he had ruined the cards. But afterward, she let him keep them. Michael didn't think they were ruined. He thought the kings and queens looked pretty with orange and purple faces.

Anyway, Michael always kept his suitcase under his bed where he could get it right away, in case Miss Finch came to take him someplace else again. Miss Finch was his social worker. A social worker was somebody who helped you when you didn't have a mother or father.

Miss Finch had been his social worker ever since he could remember, so he guessed that made her kind of like "family." And he liked her a lot. Every time she picked him up in her car (it looked like a big yellow beetle) to drive him from one foster home to another, they always stopped at Jack in the Box for hamburgers and Cokes.

Of course, Miss Finch wasn't really his family. But she's the only kind of "family" I've got, Michael reminded himself. Foster "moms" and foster "dads" were okay (except some were sort of mean), but they didn't really belong to you. You never knew when they were going to tell you it was time to pack your suitcase again.

He reached down and felt the familiar worn leather once more. It's the *realest* thing in my life, my old brown suitcase. The one thing that really belongs to me!

He was too tired to feel mad anymore. He curled his fingers tightly around the handle, and finally he fell asleep.

The next day, he was playing Candyland with Tina, one of his foster sisters. She was just three years old, so she only knew how to play baby games. Michael had just landed on the green square next to the Rainbow Trail when he looked out the front window and saw Miss Finch's car drive up.

Michael jumped up quickly to go get his suitcase.

"Watch out—you almost knocked over the game!" Tina yelled after him, but Michael didn't pay any attention. He was trying to find his tow truck and his deck of cards to pack them in his suitcase.

Miss Finch smiled when she hurried in. (Miss Finch always hurried in and hurried out.) "No, no, Michael— you don't have to pack your things this time," she told him in her in-a-hurry voice. "Just run out and hop in the car. I have a surprise for you."

"Are we going to Jack in the Box?"

"No—you'll see."

Michael had to take twice as many steps to keep up with Miss Finch as they ran out and got into the car. "Here we go," Miss Finch sang out as she turned the key and sent the yellow beetle scurrying along the street.

They rode downtown, to the building that was called the County Bureau of Adoptions. Michael remembered coming here with Miss Finch lots of times, sitting on the hard leather chair in her office while she looked through the pile of papers on her desk.

But afterward, she always took him to a new foster home. So why hadn't she let him bring his suitcase along? Maybe this time I'm going to have to leave my suitcase behind. Maybe that's the surprise. A surprise didn't always mean something good.

What's going to happen to me now? he wanted to ask. But he was scared the answer would be something he didn't want to know.

"Come along," said Miss Finch as she parked the car and got out. Michael jumped out and hurried along beside her.

They went into the building and walked down a long empty hall. Miss Finch's high wooden heels made a loud noise like somebody hammering. Michael was afraid to make noise in such a quiet place. He was glad he was wearing his sneakers, but he walked on his tiptoes besides, just to make sure.

They came to a door at the end of the hall. It wasn't the way to Miss Finch's office. The surprise must be behind the door.

Michael swallowed hard. I hope it's a *good* surprise.

Miss Finch opened the door. Michael peeked inside. There were red and yellow, blue and green balloons and bright-colored paper streamers hung all across the ceiling. Ten or twelve boys and girls sat at a big table covered with a red-and-white peppermint-striped paper tablecloth.

The boys and girls stared at Michael as he came in. Michael saw that each one had a little birthday cake.

"It's a surprise party," explained Miss Finch. "We thought some of you children who've been with us all of your lives should have a special birthday party." She took Michael's hand. "Come on—let's find your place."

Michael held back. The other boys and girls at the table were still staring at him, the way new foster brothers and sisters always had whenever he'd moved into a new foster home. But if I sit down with them, Michael thought, I'll get a birthday cake, too.

He was right. Miss Finch led him over to the empty chair at the table, where there was a birthday cake with seven candles. "Happy birthday, Michael," she said.

He looked around. The girl across from him only had five candles on her cake. But the big boy next to him had *thirteen* on his.

The boy grinned at Michael. "Looks like I'm the oldest dude here," he said.

"Happy birthday," said Michael.

Miss Finch and two other ladies (Michael guessed they were social workers, too) walked around the table to light the candles on the cakes. Then one of the other ladies turned out the big ceiling light.

"*Ooo-ooh!*" Michael gasped with the other children. He had never seen so many candles lit all at once. Everybody giggled at each other across the table. In the flickering light, their faces looked like shining moons.

Michael giggled along with the others. The candle-light made everyone seem friendly. "I wish we didn't have to blow out our candles," he said.

"Me too," said the little girl across from him.

"If we don't, we can't eat our cake," the big boy reminded them.

"And look—there's fudge ripple, besides!" said a boy at the other end of the table as one of the ladies started scooping ice cream from a carton.

Everybody took big breaths and got ready to blow. "Don't forget to make a wish, Michael," said Miss Finch.

There was one thing Michael wanted more than anything else in the world. He squeezed his eyes shut, concentrated on his wish, and blew as hard as he could.

He opened his eyes. He had blown out all the candles on his cake in just one breath. Maybe his wish would come true.

Then he looked around. Most of the other kids had blown out all their candles, too. And I bet they all wished the same thing I did, thought Michael.

He had to hold back his tears again. With a whole roomful of foster kids all wishing they would get adopted, what chance did his wish have?

New Mom

A *dopt* me?" Michael repeated after Miss Finch. When he'd seen Miss Finch coming again, he was sure it was time to move to another foster home. But instead, Miss Finch had reached into her purse and shown him a color snapshot of a smiling lady in a green sweater.

"Her name is Miss Graham, and she thinks she'd like to adopt you," Miss Finch had explained.

Michael stared at the picture. The lady looked sort of old (her hair was gray and she had some wrinkles), but she didn't look mean.

"I'm going to take you over to meet her today," said Miss Finch. "We'll see how you feel about each other."

Maybe the lady won't like me, Michael worried. Maybe I won't like her. I hope she'll want to keep me, and I hope I'll want to stay. He gave his old brown suitcase a kick. I'm tired of packing and going some-place else all the time!

Michael rode with Miss Finch to a quiet street of small wood houses with porches looking out on grassy front yards. Miss Finch parked the car in front of a snug green-and-white house with the biggest front yard Michael had ever seen.

It looked like a perfect place to play. There was even a swing made from an old tire hanging from the branch of a big tree. But Michael didn't see any children.

"Does this lady have some other children?" he asked.

"No," answered Miss Finch. "But I've talked to her a long time, and I think she'd be a good mother for you."

My own mom, thought Michael. Not just a foster mother. A *real* one!

"Miss Graham doesn't have a husband, either," Miss Finch went on. "She isn't married."

This lady sounds different, thought Michael. Maybe she isn't going to be an ordinary mother.

Then he thought about himself, about being a foster child and getting bounced around all his life from one place to another. I guess I'm not an ordinary kid, either.

"C'mon," said Miss Finch. "Let's see how you two hit it off."

Michael let Miss Finch hold his hand as they walked

up to the house. It was funny—he felt more shy than all those times when Miss Finch had taken him into strange new foster homes.

A woman opened the door and called out to them, "Hello! Come in!" She wasn't wearing a green sweater, but Michael could tell by her smile (and her gray hair and glasses) that she was the lady in the picture.

Miss Finch introduced them, and the lady shook his hand. "I'm glad to meet you, Michael."

Michael opened his mouth to answer, but his voice wouldn't come out.

"Are you feeling scared?" Miss Graham asked him. "*I* am."

What's *she* scared of? wondered Michael.

"I'm going to leave you two alone to get acquainted," said Miss Finch. "I'll be back to pick you up in a little while, Michael."

Michael watched Miss Finch hurry down the walk and get into the yellow beetle. *No, don't go!* he wanted to holler after her. He didn't want her to leave him alone with the lady.

It was different those other times, when she left him at foster homes. At least there were always other foster kids there.

"Don't worry." Miss Graham smiled at him. "She'll be back soon. While you're waiting, you can look around the house if you want to."

He *did* want to see the house—especially if maybe he was going to come and live here.

"First, here's the kitchen." She led him into a sunny yellow room and held out a fat round jar with a happy clown face painted on it. "And here's the cookie jar."

She lifted the lid and Michael scooped out a handful of chocolate chip cookies. Maybe I'm going to like this house after all, he thought as he took a crunchy bite and let the sweet bits of chocolate melt on his tongue.

In the living room, there was a piano and a color TV, and beside the fireplace a little decorated Christmas tree! Summer isn't even over, puzzled Michael.

Miss Graham turned on the colored lights on the tree. "I feel like Christmas more than once a year, don't you?"

Michael nodded, but he wasn't sure. He would have to think about it.

Next, she showed him a room that was all books and pictures, with a desk and typewriter in the middle of it. "This is where I work."

"What kind of work?"

"Writing stories." Michael didn't know mothers did that kind of work.

"Now, would you like to see your room?" she asked him.

"*My* room?"

"If you decide to come and live here."

Michael wiped his cookie crumbs onto his jeans as he stood in the doorway and stared into the room. Miss Graham smiled. "It's all right—go in and look around."

Inside, there was a bed, and a desk and chair, and a shelf of books and games. Some were his favorites—checkers and chess, Monopoly and Stratego. (He had learned to play lots of games on rainy days with his foster brothers and sisters.)

There was even a big map of the world on the wall. *His* room? Everything?

"I never had my own room before," he said. He wondered how he'd feel in a room without any other kids.

"It's good to have a place where you can be alone when you want to be," said Miss Graham.

"Do you live all alone in this house?" he asked her.

"Yes."

"Don't you get scared sometimes?"

"Not very."

"Don't you get lonely?"

"Sometimes. But it's all right to be lonely sometimes." She looked at Michael without smiling. "That's not why I want to adopt you. I'd adopt a dog or a cat or a canary for that."

"Didn't you ever get married?"

"No. I almost did—twice. Once, it was not the right time. The other time, it was not the right person."

"I almost got adopted twice," said Michael.

"I know," said Miss Graham.

Once it had been in a house where he didn't want to stay, because the people yelled at him all the time. Why did they want to adopt a boy just to yell at him?

The other time he was almost adopted, the people had been nice. Michael had wanted to stay, but the people changed their minds and couldn't keep him anymore.

They had tried to explain to him that it wasn't his fault. So had Miss Finch. But Michael still thought maybe he'd done something wrong. He still wondered about it sometimes. Only then he'd feel like crying again, so he'd make himself think of something else.

Now, standing in "his" room with the new lady who

wanted to adopt him, Michael looked down and saw his shoelace was untied. I hope she doesn't notice! Maybe she won't want to adopt me if she finds out I'm seven and can't tie my shoelaces good yet.

Instead, she suddenly asked him, "How would you like to help me wash the car?"

He had never washed a car before, but now that he thought about it, it was something he'd always wanted to do. "Okay!"

"Better take off your shoes and socks, and roll up your jeans so you won't get too wet," she said.

Michael stopped worrying about his shoelaces, pulled off his shoes and socks, and rolled up his jeans. They carried a pail of water and some soap and rags outside to where a big red car was parked in the driveway.

"You can start scrubbing the bottom while I scrub the top." Miss Graham handed him a soft soapy rag. "You have the big job. The bottom is the dirtiest part."

Squatting beside the car, Michael stared into the chrome hubcaps at the reflection of the sunny day and the street of friendly houses where maybe he was going to live. He felt scared and excited at the same time.

But right now, I better do my job! The lady was right.

He had to scrub hard to wash away the spatters of mud on the big red fenders. Where did she go in her car? If he came here to live, would she take him with her?

Water spilled on the ground around him, and his bare feet on the wet grass felt good. When the car was covered with soap and water, the lady handed him the hose. "Get ready," she warned. "I'm going to turn it on."

Michael held on to the hose and pointed it at the car. But suddenly the hose leaped right out of his hands. *Whoosh!* The water squirted out—all over the lady! Her face and hair were all wet!

17

"*Oh!*" Michael caught his breath. She's *mad*! She won't adopt me now.

Miss Graham shook the water out of her hair and took her glasses off to wipe them on her shirt. "Hey!" she yelled. "You're supposed to give the car a bath—not me."

She was *laughing.*

Michael let out his breath. Then he picked up the hose and held it carefully as he washed the foamy soap-suds off the car until it looked as red and shiny as a fire engine.

"Now let's go for a ride," said Miss Graham.

"Where?"

"We'll think of someplace."

Michael ran in to put on his socks and his shoes. (He couldn't tie the laces good enough—there was no use trying.) Miss Graham put on her green sweater. "Now you look like your picture," said Michael.

But as soon as they were settled in the car, she *noticed.* "Better tie your shoelaces—you might trip."

He had to tell her the truth. "I can't do it right."

"Never mind—I'll show you later." She reached over and tied them for him quickly. "Right now, I've thought of someplace for us to go."

It was all right! His shoelaces weren't important. She didn't mind at all.

She turned the key to start the motor, then pressed a button. The whole top of the car lifted up and *disappeared.* "I hope you like fresh air," she said.

Michael had never ridden in a car without a top before. He liked looking up at the sky, watching the thin white trail of a jet roaring high over his head.

After a while, they pulled up to a hot dog stand. "I bet I know one thing about boys," Miss Graham said. "They're always hungry."

They sat at a table outdoors, alongside the busy street where they could watch the people and cars go by. Miss Graham squirted gobs of mustard and catsup on her hot dog and licked the drippings off her fingers.

She smiled at Michael. "The messier it is, the better it tastes—right?"

"Right!" Michael smiled back, squirting gobs of mustard and catsup on his hot dog and licking the drippings off his fingers, too. He opened the little paper cup of salt and sprinkled it on his french fries.

As soon as he took the first bite, a small brown bird flew down and landed on the table beside him. "I think he wants a bite of your french fry," said Miss Graham.

19

Michael broke off a crumb, but when he held it out to the sparrow, it flew away. "He got scared." Michael was disappointed.

"He'll be back. I think city birds like french fries better than worms."

Michael made a face. "Me, too!"

Just then, the sparrow hopped back on the table beside him. "Shhh—don't move," whispered Miss Graham. Michael stopped chewing his hot dog. The sparrow hopped closer and closer, then quickly picked up the piece of french fry and flew away with it.

"He's going someplace quiet to eat," Miss Graham said.

"Where no other bird can take his french fry away from him," answered Michael, remembering the time one of his foster brothers had grabbed a Hershey bar right out of his hand.

If he came to live with this lady, he wouldn't have any foster brothers and sisters to fight with. Only who would he play with? "Do you know any children?" he asked.

"Yes," she answered, smiling. "And there are two boys who live just down the street."

That's good, thought Michael.

They finished eating. "We better go now," she said.

"Miss Finch will be coming for you."

All the way back in the car, Michael stared up at the sky, wondering, What's going to happen now?

Miss Finch was already at the house, waiting for them. "Well, how did you two get along?" she asked as they walked up to the porch together.

"We had hot dogs," said Michael. "And I gave a sparrow one of my french fries."

"That sounds like fun," said Miss Finch.

"And I helped wash the car."

"It looks beautiful."

"Michael and I have just begun to get to know each other," said Miss Graham.

"Do I have to go back to the foster home now?" Michael asked.

Miss Finch looked like she was thinking about it. "Do you want to go back?" she asked.

Michael nodded. "I have to get my suitcase." He smiled at Miss Graham, and she smiled back. "What should I call you?" he asked.

"You can call me 'mom'—if you want to."

He had called all of his foster mothers "mom." Maybe now, at last, he was going to have a *real* mom.

"I want to," he said.

Friends

Michael moved into his new house and his new room. He unpacked his suitcase, putting his clothes neatly away in the closet and setting his tow truck and his deck of cards carefully on the shelf beside the games and books.

Then he slid his suitcase under his bed where he always kept it. Only this time, he thought, maybe I can put it away, high up on the shelf in the closet. Maybe I won't need it anymore.

No! Michael shook his head. I was *almost* adopted before. My new mom might change her mind, too. I'm going to have to remember that!

But it wouldn't do any good to sit around and worry about it. He pulled on his warm red sweater and ran out to play in his new front yard.

Two boys across the street were passing a football back and forth. My new front yard is perfect for playing football, thought Michael. It's almost as big as a real gridiron.

"Hi!" he hollered to the boys. "Want to come over and play in my yard?" He hoped they would want to be his friends. He was used to having lots of kids to play with.

The dark-haired boy hollered back, "Sure!" He started across the street, jerking his head for his friend to follow him. "C'mon, Pete."

The blond boy shrugged. "What for?" But he strolled across the street after him.

Michael waved them both into his yard. "C'mon in—my name's Michael."

"Hi—I'm Tony," said the friendly boy, whose hair and eyes were as black as Michael's. "And he's Peter."

Peter stood back, juggling the football in his hands, scowling at Michael. "I thought the lady who moved in here didn't have any kids."

"She's going to adopt me," explained Michael. *Maybe,* he thought; he didn't say that part out loud.

"How come you have to be adopted?" Peter asked, still scowling.

"My mother and father couldn't keep me when I was

born," said Michael. He wished they would start throwing the ball again, and let him play too.

"That must be rough," said Tony.

"It's okay—I have a new mom now," answered Michael. *Maybe.*

"That's good," said Tony. He held up his hands. "C'mon, Pete—throw one."

Michael watched the ball sail out of Peter's hands into Tony's. Tony grinned at him. "Want to catch one?"

Michael's face lit up. "Okay!"

Tony pointed across the yard. "Go stand over there."

Michael ran over and stood ready to catch the ball. Tony sent it spiraling toward him in a high arc against the sky. Michael held out his hands. *Ow!* The hard leather stung his palms. He let the ball drop to the ground.

"Pick it up!" shouted Tony.

"Throw it back!" hollered Peter.

Michael grabbed up the ball and threw it as hard as he could. The ball wobbled through the air and landed halfway across the yard.

I'm sunk, Michael thought. If I don't know how to throw the ball and I can't catch it either, they won't play with me. They'll take their football and go away.

"You're not holding the ball right," Tony yelled at him. "C'mere—I'll show you."

Michael ran over. Tony held the ball to show him. "See—grip it here, by the laces. Okay?"

Michael nodded.

"Now try another pass."

Peter ran across the yard, holding out his arms. "Let's see you send one to me."

Michael stretched his fingers to try and hold the ball the way Tony showed him, and he sent it into the air. It didn't wobble quite as much, but it didn't even go as far as the first time he'd tried.

Peter scowled at him again. "How old are you, anyway?"

"Seven," answered Michael.

"No wonder! You're too little to play football."

"I am not!" protested Michael.

"We're both nine," explained Tony. "But that's okay—you'll learn."

"In a couple of years," scoffed Peter.

Tony picked up the football. "I'll throw a pass to Peter," he told Michael. "Watch how he catches it."

Peter caught the ball close against his body. "See?

That way it doesn't sting your hands so much," Tony explained.

"Okay—here comes one at you!" Peter yelled from across the yard. Michael watched the ball come shooting through the air toward him. He could already feel the sting of the hard leather on his palms. He ducked. The ball bounced to the ground.

"Forget it!" Peter turned away. "Come on, Tony—this isn't any fun."

"Ah, let's give him one more chance, Pete."

Peter looked back. "Some other time maybe. We have to get over to the playground for the game."

"Right." Tony picked up the ball and ran out of the yard after Peter. "See you later, Mike," he called back over his shoulder.

Michael didn't answer. He stood in his yard, watching the two boys go down the street, passing the football smoothly between them.

It isn't fair! he thought. It's not my fault I'm only seven.

But when his mom took him to his new school, all the boys and girls in his class were seven, too.

"Do you like to play football?" Michael asked Albert one day at recess. Albert was kind of fat, but he was one of the fastest runners on the playground. He sat at the same table with Michael in class, and they were beginning to be friends.

"Benny has a new football," said Albert. "I'll ask him to bring it to school tomorrow." Benny was Albert's other friend. Benny was the smallest boy in class, and he was also the smartest.

"It's because Benny's Chinese," Albert had explained to Michael. "Chinese people are very smart."

Albert was Mexican, and he was pretty smart too. He could speak Spanish as well as he could speak English.

The next day Benny brought his football, and at recess Michael and Albert and Benny hurried out to the playground. Michael ran across the yard. "I'm going out for a pass! Throw me the ball!" he hollered over his shoulder at Benny.

Benny threw the ball. It wobbled all over the place. "That's because you're not holding it right," explained Michael. "C'mere—I'll show you."

Albert and Benny ran over. Michael held the ball the way Tony had shown him. "Try it," he told Benny.

"I'll go out for the pass this time," hollered Albert, as he ran across the yard. Benny threw the ball, but Albert dropped it. *"Ow!"*

Michael winced too. "Sure stings, huh!"

Albert blew on his hand and shook it up and down, trying to make the sting go away.

"I'll show you how to catch it," said Michael. He cradled the ball in his arms against his body the way he'd seen Peter do it. "Like this. Then it won't sting your hands so much and you won't drop it."

They practiced throwing the ball back and forth. I'm getting to be a pretty good passer—almost, thought Michael.

The bell rang. Recess was over. They had to go back inside.

"We'll practice some more tomorrow," said Michael.

"Right," said Albert. "Thanks!"

"Yeah—thanks," echoed Benny.

Michael felt better. Now he had two friends who were just his age.

One day after school, his mom took him to meet another new friend. "His name is Henry," she said, as she parked the car in front of a spanking-clean white house, where a flock of blackbirds pecked at the grass under a magnolia tree.

"Is Henry older than me?" asked Michael.

"Yes—a good deal older."

"Peter and Tony showed me how to play football," said Michael.

His mom smiled. "I'm afraid Henry is a little *too* old for football."

They walked around to the backyard, where an old man was busy at a workbench. He had white hair thin as thread, and a face as brown and leathery as Michael's old suitcase.

The man pushed his glasses up from his nose and smiled as he saw them coming. "Anytime anything breaks in the neighborhood, folks bring it over to see if I can fix it. Most times, I can." He gave Michael a wink. "You can fix just about anything, if you want to bad enough."

As Henry took them into the house, Michael smelled baked apple and cinnamon. "Hope you're in the mood for some hot apple pie," said Henry. "I have one just ready to come out of the oven."

"You know how to bake a pie?" asked Michael.

"Sure do. Learned how to cook in the Navy."

"I thought you learned how to sail a ship in the Navy," said Michael, surprised.

"Already knew that," said Henry. "And how to build one, too."

After they had their pie, Henry showed Michael a miniature ship with white sails billowing from three tall masts—inside a bottle!

Henry smiled. "Looks tricky, doesn't it? Well, it isn't. Just takes time and patience, and a steady hand."

"But how did you build it inside the bottle?" asked Michael.

"That's the easy part," said Henry. "I didn't. You build it outside—then you slide it into the bottle, with the masts and sails down. After that, you work at it with a wire and raise the masts and sails back up—and there you have it."

Michael looked at the little sailing ship and imagined being on a real one, sailing across the ocean to some faraway place. "How'd you like to take that little ship home with you?" Henry asked him.

"You mean you're going to give it to me?"

Henry placed the ship in the bottle carefully in Michael's hands. "Something to remember your old sailor friend by."

"*Thanks!*" breathed Michael. It was fun having a friend like Henry, who knew how to do so many things.

Back home in his room, he set Henry's ship on the bookshelf, next to his tow truck and deck of cards. I can show Tony and Peter when they come to my house again.

If they come again, he corrected himself quickly.

Michael went outside and looked up and down the street. But Tony and Peter weren't anywhere around. He climbed into the tire hanging from the big tree, and swung back and forth under the leafy branches.

This was his favorite place to be by himself. This swing is my friend too, he thought. And so's this tree . . . and my front yard . . . and all the houses on my new street . . .

"*Mee-ow.*" A skinny black cat rubbed against his leg.

"Hello, cat," said Michael. "Where'd you come from?"

"*Mee-ow.*"

"Don't you belong to anybody?"

"*Mee-ow.*"

Michael picked up the cat and held its warm furry body against his cheek.

"Purr-rrr-rr . . ."

Michael laughed. "You sound like a motorboat. I guess that's what I'll call you. Okay?"

"Purr-rrr-rr . . ."

"Maybe I'll *adopt* you, like my mom's going to adopt me. Okay?"

"Mee-ow."

"Then you'll really *belong* to me—huh, cat!"

"Purr-rrr-rr . . ."

Michael grinned. "C'mon, Motorboat—let's go ask mom."

Family

One day Michael's teacher said, "I want each of you to write about your family."

Michael sat at his table, wondering what to write. He had had many families—different foster mothers and fathers, and foster brothers and sisters. But none of them was his real family. Now, he only had his new mom—and she wasn't really his mother. Not yet.

Michael chewed on the end of his pencil and stared at the blank piece of paper in front of him. He looked across the table at Albert, busily writing. Albert had lots of family to write about—a mother and father, three brothers, and four sisters!

I bet everybody else in the room has a regular family, with a real mother and father, thought Michael.

"How do you spell 'brother'?" a girl asked the teacher.

"B-r-o-t-h-e-r," answered the teacher.

"How do you spell 'sister'?" asked a boy.

"S-i-s-t-e-r."

Michael frowned. Everybody has a brother or sister, too. Except me. I don't even have a father.

He could write about his new mom. She was fun. How many mothers kept a Christmas tree around to turn on whenever they felt like it? And when he'd asked her if he could keep Motorboat, she'd said yes right away.

He hoped she was going to be his real mother someday. (But she might change her mind. He had to keep remembering that.)

Still, a mother was just a mother. A mother wasn't a family.

He bit down on his pencil. Any minute now, the teacher would ask him why he wasn't writing his paper. He didn't want to say out loud that he didn't have a family. He thought of a question, and raised his hand.

"Yes, Michael?"

"How do you spell 'family'?"

"F-a-m-i-l-y," answered the teacher.

Michael carefully printed the words "My Family" at the top of his paper. He could make up a family. He

would have a mother and father, two brothers, and
maybe one sister.

A girl in the back of the room raised her hand. "How
do you spell 'Grandma'?"

"G-r-a-n-d-m-a."

And he would have a grandma and a grandpa, too. He looked across the room at Benny. Benny's grandmother and grandfather lived right in the same house with him.

I'll *have* to make up a family, Michael decided. He started to write. "I have a new mother who is very nice." At least that much was true.

Then the bell rang. School was over for the day. Michael was glad. Now he wouldn't have to lie.

But when the teacher saw his unfinished paper, she told him, "You may take it home with you to finish, Michael. That will be your homework."

That night at dinner, Michael didn't feel like eating—even though his mom had cooked his favorite, spaghetti. He'd gotten used to sitting in his corner of the bright yellow kitchen. He liked all the things his mom had put up on the wall beside his place—pictures of animals and plants they'd seen on their Saturday adventures in the nearby desert (he liked the roadrunner best), and a map of the United States (by now, he'd learned almost all fifty state capitals from looking at the map every morning at breakfast).

He and his mom had made dinner a special time, when they told each other about their day. But tonight

Michael didn't feel like talking, either. He sat with his elbow on the table, poking his fork at the spaghetti on his plate.

"What's the matter?" his mom asked.

"I don't want to do my homework." Michael told her about the paper he was supposed to write.

"You have a grandpa who lives in Florida," said his mom.

"I do?" Michael was surprised.

"My father is your grandpa," his mom explained. "Maybe someday we can take a trip so you can meet him."

"Do I have a grandma, too?" asked Michael.

His mom shook her head. "No, your grandma died before you came here. It's too bad, honey—she would have loved you very much."

Michael frowned. "I don't have enough to write my paper."

"Don't worry—eat your spaghetti," said his mom. "Then, first thing after dinner, you can help me write a letter to Kim Soo and Kim Joong."

"Who?" asked Michael.

"They're my two foster children in Korea," said his mom. "That means they're your foster brothers."

"Hooray!" cheered Michael. "I don't have to make up brothers."

He gobbled up his spaghetti while she explained. "Kim Soo is eleven years old, and Kim Joong is thirteen. They both like to play baseball. You can write and tell them you like to play football."

"I like baseball, too," said Michael.

As soon as they finished dinner, they went into Michael's room. His mom showed him Korea on his map of the world. I bet nobody else in school has two brothers who live across the ocean, thought Michael. His mom was always surprising him. She sure was different from other mothers.

"After we finish writing the letter, I'm going to do my homework," he said.

Next morning before he went to school, Michael gave Motorboat a fresh saucer of milk. Then he put a drop of water and a piece of lemon leaf into the ant farm his mom had bought for him. As he watched the ants scurry out of their tunnels to nibble on the leaf, he thought of something more to write on his paper.

As soon as he got to school, he gave his paper to the teacher. The teacher read it. Then she read it again— out loud to the whole class.

My Family

I have a new mother who is very nice. And I have a black cat who makes a noise like a motorboat, so that is what I call her.
My grandma is in heaven and my grandpa is in Florida. And I have two big brothers who play baseball in Korea.
I also have six ants.

"My goodness, Michael," said the teacher. "You have an interesting family."

"Thanks," said Michael.

"There's only one thing," said the teacher. "The correct way to spell 'aunt' is a-*u*-n-t."

Michael smiled. "That's not the way to spell the ants in *my* family." He explained about his ant farm.

"You have a *very* interesting family, Michael," said the teacher.

After school Albert and Benny walked partway home with him, so they could all play with Benny's new Frisbee.

"You wrote the best paper in the whole class," said Albert, as Michael jumped up to catch the Frisbee before it sailed into the street.

"You're lucky," said Benny, as Michael sailed the Frisbee back to him. "We only have ordinary aunts in my family."

Michael felt proud. He still kind of wished he had a regular family like everybody else. But he liked being different, too.

He waved so long to Albert and Benny at the corner and turned down his street. The first thing he saw was Miss Finch's car parked in front of his house. Michael's stomach turned over. She's going to take me away to another foster home!

He wished he could hide someplace. But it was getting cold out, and pretty soon it would get dark. Miss Finch would probably hang around forever, waiting to take him away.

Maybe he could sneak inside the house and hide in his room. That would be better. At least it would be warm, and Motorboat would be there to keep him company.

He went up the front walk quietly and tiptoed to the front door to listen. He couldn't hear anything. Slowly, he turned the knob and opened the door, hoping it wouldn't make any noise.

His mom and Miss Finch were talking in the kitchen.

41

He smelled the good smell of fresh coffee. "When will Michael be home?" he heard Miss Finch ask. She had come to get him, all right!

If only he could tiptoe into his room without being seen. But as soon as he took the first step—*cre-eak!* The floor squeaked under his sneakers.

"Michael?" called his mom.

It was no use. Now his mom would come looking for him. He gave up and went into the kitchen.

Miss Finch smiled at him. "Hello, Michael."

"H'lo."

"How are you getting along?"

"Fine!" he answered in a loud voice. Even if she tries to take me away, I won't go. She couldn't pick me up and carry me. I'm too big now.

Miss Finch looked at his spelling and arithmetic papers that his mom had put up on the kitchen bulletin board. He had four wrong in arithmetic, but he had only one wrong in spelling.

"That's pretty good," said Miss Finch.

Motorboat came into the kitchen and meowed. "That's my cat," said Michael. "Her name is Motorboat."

"Hello, Motorboat," said Miss Finch.

She hasn't said anything about taking me away, thought Michael. Maybe she came to tell me I'm *adopted* now! "Do you want to see my room?" he asked.

Miss Finch finished her coffee and got up from the table. "I'd like to very much."

Michael took her into his room and showed her the ship in the bottle from Henry. "I have a *lot* of new friends," he said, thinking about Albert and Benny at school, and Tony and Peter down the street who maybe were going to be his friends.

Miss Finch smiled. "It sounds as though you're getting along fine, all right."

Michael's mom came to the doorway. "We're both getting along fine," she said.

"That's good to hear," said Miss Finch.

"Am I adopted now?" asked Michael.

Miss Finch shook her head. "No, Michael—not yet. You have to wait a whole year."

Michael held on tightly to his little ship in the bottle. "A whole year?" By then, his mom might change her mind and not want to keep him anymore. He remembered the family he'd liked who had almost adopted him. Even nice people change their minds if they want to.

His mom came in and gave him a hug. "Don't worry," she said. "The year's going faster than you think."

Superman

Michael pulled the bright red-and-blue costume on over his jeans and T-shirt, and smiled at himself in the mirror. He stood with his legs spread apart, his fists on his hips, the red cape jaunty on his shoulders, the big red S bravely on his chest.

He wasn't Michael anymore. He was SUPERMAN!

Motorboat rubbed against his legs and purred. "You're not supposed to know me, cat," said Michael, disappointed.

Then he remembered. He reached into the orange-and-black box on his bed, found the red Superman mask, and slipped it over his face. He stared down at his cat through the little eyeholes. Motorboat stopped purring and backed away into the corner.

Michael grinned. "That's better."

He could hardly wait for the Halloween carnival at school. I bet nobody will know who I am!

He slipped off his mask and got down beside his cat. "It's all right, Motorboat—it's only me."

"*Mee-ow.*" Motorboat came out of the corner and sniffed at him. Michael scratched her soft furry ears. "I wish you could come to the Halloween carnival with me. I bet everybody would be scared of a black cat like you."

When it was time for the carnival, Michael's mom drove him to the school. The playground was decorated as if for a party, with orange balloons and twisted orange and black paper streamers. A row of game booths was set up along the fence.

It was crowded with mothers and fathers and with children in costumes. The first person Michael met was another Superman. They stared at each other from behind their masks. The other Superman was shorter than Michael. In fact, he was shorter than almost any other kid around.

"Benny? Is that you?" asked Michael.

Benny flipped up his mask and grinned. "Hey, Michael—is that you?"

Michael lifted his mask and looked around. "Where's Albert?"

Benny shrugged. "I haven't seen him yet. I think he's Batman."

They looked around at the other kids. There were about ten other Supermen, about twenty Batmen, and a jillion ballerinas and witches.

"I'm going to look for Albert. See you later," said Benny, sliding his mask back over his eyes.

"See you," said Michael. He decided to leave his mask off, so he could see better to play the games. He didn't care anymore if the other kids saw who he was. Winning a prize was more important.

"What game do you want to play?" asked his mom, coming up beside him.

"All of them!" exclaimed Michael.

They counted ten different game booths. His mom bought ten tickets, so he could try every game.

The first booth was decorated like the others with orange balloons and crepe paper, and cardboard black cats and witches. Inside the booth there was a stack of bottles. The man in charge held up three baseballs.

"Knock down one bottle and you win a prize. Knock 'em all down and you win a big one." He pointed to a shelf of giant stuffed animals.

Michael got in line behind three other boys, and watched while they took their turns. The first boy only knocked down one bottle (he won a plastic snake), but both the other boys knocked down three bottles (they each won a plastic gorilla).

When it was Michael's turn, he threw the ball as hard as he could—but he missed. His second ball missed, too. "Go easy, son," said the man in the booth. "Take better aim."

Michael aimed carefully and threw the last ball. *Bop!* He hit the top bottle—but it didn't fall down. "Too bad, young fella," said the man. "You didn't throw it hard enough that time."

Michael thought about the way Tony had shown him how to throw a football. I wish he'd show me how to throw a baseball, too!

Next, he tried the Dart Game. But he didn't break any balloons, so he still didn't win a prize. He tried the Penny Pitch, HopScotch, and Tic-Tac-Toe, one game after another. But he didn't win anything.

He felt *dumb*. Boy, some Superman *I* am! It seemed like every kid he saw had won something. One boy had even won a big stuffed dinosaur. Superman Benny and Batman Albert came running up to him.

"Look what I won throwing darts," said Benny. He dangled a plastic spider in Michael's face. I don't want a silly old spider anyway, thought Michael. I'm going to win something better.

Albert had a stuffed polka-dotted snake wrapped around his neck. "How'd you win *that*?" Michael asked.

"I saved up all my prize tickets."

So far, Michael didn't have any prize tickets to save up. "What did you win?" Benny asked him.

49

"Nothing—yet," Michael had to admit. "But I'm going to win a really good prize. You'll see."

"Good luck," said Benny.

"See you later," said Albert.

Michael only had one ticket left, and only one more game to try—the Fishbowls. He walked over to the booth. Some of the crepe-paper decorations were torn and the balloons were starting to shrivel up.

He looked around. The playground wasn't crowded anymore. The carnival's almost over, and I didn't win a prize!

He looked at the fishbowls lined up in a row, with a baby goldfish swimming in each one. All you had to do was throw a Ping-Pong ball into one of the bowls and you won the fish.

A real live goldfish would be a better prize than a plastic spider or a polka-dotted snake.

He threw the first ball. It bounced off the table and rolled on the ground. "That's all right, son—you have two more chances," said the man in the booth.

"You can still win," said his mom.

"I know," said Michael. But his second ball landed between two fishbowls and stuck there.

"Awww—too bad!" said a lady standing behind him, waiting for her little girl's turn.

"Luck of the game," said the man in the booth.

"You still have another chance," said his mom.

"I know," said Michael again, but he didn't sound so sure this time. He looked at each fish. Which one would he like to have? He saw a bright gold one with a big beautiful tail. *That* one, he decided.

He aimed his last ball—very carefully—and threw it. *Plop!* It landed right in the bowl. "I win! I win!" Michael jumped up and down, clapping his hands. "Hooray for me! Hooray for me!"

His mom and the lady and little girl behind him clapped for him, too. "You've won yourself a fine prize," said the man in the booth.

"I hope the Ping-Pong ball didn't hurt my fish," worried Michael.

"Don't worry—he's fine," said the man, putting it into a little bag of water for Michael to carry home.

"I'm going to call him Charlie," Michael said. "Charlie's a good name for a fish." He looked around for Albert and Benny to show them his fish, but he didn't see them anywhere.

"They must have gone home," said his mom. "The carnival's over."

"It's all right," said Michael. "I can tell them about Charlie tomorrow."

On the way home, Michael and his mom stopped at the dime store to buy a fishbowl for Charlie to live in and some green plants to put in the bottom of the bowl for Charlie to nibble on.

At home, Michael's mom fixed a place for Charlie's bowl on the kitchen table. "Where Charlie can feel part of the family," she said.

Now I have some more family to write about, thought Michael. He filled the bowl with fresh water, put in the green plants, then opened the plastic bag to let Charlie swim into his new home.

"I won the best prize of all," he said.

"Congratulations, Superman," said his mom.

First Christmas

It was a frosty December day. As Michael walked home from school, with his nose buried in the collar of his jacket, he counted three cars with Christmas trees tied on top and one with a tree sticking out of the trunk in back.

As soon as he got home, his mom said, "Let's go get our tree tonight."

"We already have a Christmas tree." Michael reminded her about the little decorated tree by the fireplace. Now he always asked his mom to turn it on whenever he felt like Christmas. She was right. He felt like it lots more than once a year.

"When it's really Christmas," said his mom, "it's time to put up a big tree."

After dinner, they put on their coats and started out the door. "Don't forget the car keys," said Michael. He always had to remind her about things like that.

"We won't need the car," she answered.

"How will we get the tree home?"

"You'll see."

They walked six blocks until they came to a vacant lot, now turned into a magic forest of Christmas trees, all shapes and sizes. Most were green, just as they grew in the mountains Michael could see from his window at school. But some had been painted pink or blue or silver.

"Christmas trees are supposed to be green," said Michael.

"There ought to be a law," said his mom.

They entered the magic forest, stepping onto a carpet of sawdust, the spicy scent of pine needles all around them. "We have to find just the right tree," his mom said.

"A big one," said Michael.

They joined the other Christmas tree shoppers, walking up and down among the rows of trees, examining each one—a tall one that was too skinny, a fat one that was too short, and one that was thick with branches on the bottom but nearly bald on top.

Finally, they found a tree that looked good. "What do you think?" asked his mom.

Michael walked all around it. "It's kind of flat on one side," he reported.

"It'll fit against the wall and leave room for our Christmas party," said his mom. "We'll invite our friends to help us trim our tree."

Michael thought about inviting his friends—Benny and Albert, of course. And Tony and Peter—would they come if he asked them? They had stopped by his yard to say hi a couple of times. But mostly they went by without stopping, passing the football between them, hurrying to the playground for a game.

While his mom paid the Christmas tree man, Michael watched the other shoppers tie their trees on top of their cars. How are we going to get our tree home? he wondered.

"Do you want your tree on top of your car or in the trunk?" asked the Christmas tree man.

"We didn't bring our car," Michael's mom explained. "We're going to carry our tree home."

"We are?" exclaimed Michael. Another one of his mom's weird ideas!

"Merry Christmas," said the man.

Michael helped his mom tip the tree over on its side. She lifted one end, and Michael lifted the other. *Oof!*

It was big. His breath came out in a frosty puff.

"Is it too heavy?" asked his mom.

"No!" said Michael. The tree was heavy, but he was strong.

They started home, carrying the tree between them, its soft branches brushing against their faces. A man smiled as he passed. "Looks like you've got yourself a fine tree."

"It's just right," said Michael.

A boy on a bicycle, with Christmas presents piled in a basket on the handlebars, rang his bell at them. A lady and a man driving by called out, "Merry Christmas!"

"I'm glad we didn't drive our tree home," said Michael. His mom's weird ideas usually turned out to be fun, after all.

When it was time for the party, Michael helped get everything ready. They hung a Christmas wreath on the front door, and lit Christmas candles on the big dining-room table where the platters of turkey and ham, salad and rolls and fruit, were spread out, making Michael's mouth water.

They put Christmas songs on the record player and popped two bowls of popcorn—one for eating and one for stringing on the tree that stood straight and tall in the corner of the living room, waiting for its trimmings of lights and ornaments.

"When's the party going to start?" asked Michael.

"Soon as everybody comes," answered his mom.

Michael wondered who of his friends would be first—Albert and Benny, or his old sailor friend Henry, or Tony and Peter? If there wasn't a game at the playground today, maybe Tony and Peter would come to their party instead.

The doorbell jingled. Michael ran to see who it was.

"Merry Christmas," said Albert.

"Are we too early?" asked Benny.

"You're right on time," said Michael.

His mom took their jackets to hang up. "Can we start stringing the popcorn now?" asked Michael.

"Good idea," she said.

She brought them needles and thread, and they settled on the floor in front of the fireplace with the two bowls of popcorn beside them. "One bowl's for eating," explained Michael, stuffing a handful of warm buttery popcorn into his mouth.

Then he took a piece of popcorn from the other bowl and tried to poke the needle and thread through it, but it broke in two. "The broken ones are for eating, too," said his mom.

It was hard to pull the thread through a piece of popcorn without breaking it, but Michael finally did it. Albert and Benny finally did it, too. The three boys began to work so hard, trying to string the popcorn, they almost forgot to eat some.

The doorbell jingled again. Michael jumped up to see if it was Tony and Peter. When he opened the door, his sailor friend Henry held out a surprise for him.

"Figured your Christmas tree could use a bird, so I carved you one. It's the spittin' image of an old sea gull friend of mine."

Michael showed it to Albert and Benny, while his mom poured Henry a glass of eggnog. They clinked their glasses together and wished each other Merry Christmas.

More friends came. Every time the doorbell jingled, Michael hoped it would be Tony and Peter. But it wasn't.

Soon the house was filled with people, some for Michael to meet for the first time. He felt a little scared, the way he used to feel each time he had to meet a new foster family. But when the tree trimming began, he forgot about being shy.

He and Albert and Benny stopped trying to string popcorn so they could help string the lights, and everyone took turns hanging ornaments on the branches. Motorboat padded in, sniffed the tree, and batted her paw at a shiny gold ball hanging from a low branch.

Michael laughed. "That's going to be Motorboat's Christmas toy."

"Until she breaks it," said his mom.

The doorbell jingled again. "Who can that be?" his mom wondered.

When Michael opened the door, there stood Tony and Peter, zipped up in warm jackets.

"Merry Christmas," said Tony.

Peter looked worried. "Are we too late for the party?"

"C'mon in!" said Michael.

He took them inside and introduced them to Albert and Benny. "We're stringing popcorn for the tree," he explained. "Want to help?"

"Sure," said Tony.

"I guess so." Peter shrugged.

It took a long time, but finally they had strung enough to wind all around the tree. The white puffs of popcorn looked like snowflakes on the green branches.

Then the boys heaped Christmas dinner on their plates and ate together on the floor in front of the fireplace. After dinner, they went through the house to turn off all the lights, leaving just the tree gleaming in the dark as everyone sang Christmas carols—"Hark, the

Herald Angels Sing" and "Silent Night" and "Good King Wenceslas."

Then, especially for Michael and Benny and Albert, they sang, "Rudolf the red-nosed reindeer had a very shiny nose . . ."

Later, when the party was over and all their friends were gone, Michael's mom brought out a small box. "I thought you'd like to put this under the tree by yourself."

Michael opened the box and unwrapped the tissue paper from the figures of Mary, Joseph, and the baby in the manger. "The very first Christmas," whispered his mom.

"When the baby Jesus was born," said Michael, as he placed the figures carefully under the tree. Someone— he couldn't remember who—had read him the story of the first Christmas.

"And this is *our* first Christmas," said his mom.

Michael stretched out on the warm rug under the soft glowing lights of the tree. Everything seemed perfect. It was Christmas. All his friends had come to their party. And best of all, he had found a new mother who wanted to adopt him.

I *hope*! he remembered quickly.

He reached up and touched the little silver bell hanging on the end of a branch. It made a small tinkling sound in the quiet house. "Every time a bell rings, an angel gets his wings," he reminded his mom.

It was a line from an old movie they liked to watch together on TV.

Christmas day, Michael raced outside with his new football. He tossed it high in the air, caught it against his chest, and ran across the yard, pretending to go for a touchdown. Playing with Albert and Benny at school every day had helped a lot.

"All *right*!" Tony came running over, wearing a new football shirt with a big number 12 on the front. Michael threw him a pass. The ball shot straight into Tony's arms.

"Hey—not bad," called Tony in surprise. He tossed a pass back to Michael, and watched him catch the ball snugly in his arms.

"I've been practicing," Michael explained proudly.

Peter came sailing down the street on his new skateboard. "Throw me one," he hollered, holding up his hands.

Michael sent the ball straight to him. Peter caught it without falling off his board. "Good shot!" he called out to Michael.

"Mike's been practicing," explained Tony.

Peter jumped off his skateboard and tossed the ball back to Michael. Michael caught it easily. Peter grinned. "Hey! Next time we have a game at the playground, d'you want to be on our team?"

"Sure!" shouted Michael.

He felt like playing a game right now, but Tony and Peter slumped down on the grass, looking unhappy. "What's the matter?" he asked.

"Christmas is over," said Peter.

"For a whole other year," said Tony.

Michael thought about how his mom turned on their little Christmas tree and played Christmas music all the time, in the middle of summer even.

He smiled. "Christmas is never over at my house."

The Biggest
Thing in the World

Michael looked far out across the gray-green Pacific Ocean. "It's so *big*!" he exclaimed.

"It's the biggest thing in the world," said his mom.

Winter was finally over, and they were having a Saturday adventure at the beach in a warm spring rain. Michael hugged his windbreaker around his neck, remembering all the Saturday adventures he'd had with his mom so far. . . .

Scrabbling up a hillside in the horse-and-farm country and stumbling over the bones of a dead fox. Then stretching out on a flat boulder soft as a couch to practice answering the meadowlarks,

and to wonder about what had killed that fox. . . .

Hiking along a dry creek bed, their eyes on the ground to watch for rocks that sparkled with flecks of shining metal, and glancing up just in time to catch sight of a jackrabbit hightailing it up the creek bed with the sun shining through his big jackrabbit ears. . . .

Walking around by people's graves in a quiet green cemetery (his mom liked cemeteries—he guessed it was because she knew so many dead people), reading the carved gravestones, and thinking about what the people were like when they were alive.

When they found a gravestone that said something special, his mom showed him how to put a piece of paper over it and rub hard across the paper with a black crayon to make a copy to keep, to help him remember. Michael had a crayon rubbing of his favorite gravestone pinned up on the wall of his room:

Whenever he looked at it, he could almost hear William S. Riley playing his banjo. I guess *I* know a lot of dead people now too, he thought. . . .

He knew a lot of new things—thanks to his new mom. They didn't just go shopping at the supermarket on Saturdays, like other kids and their mothers. His mom was different. He never knew what she was going to think of next for one of their Saturday adventures.

Now, as they walked along the surf together, he decided it was a good time to ask her the question he'd been thinking about for a long time. "How come my real mother didn't keep me?"

They sat down side by side on a piece of driftwood washed up on the shore, pulling their rain hoods snugly about their heads, feeling the wet wind on their faces. "No one knows about your real mother, Michael," said his mom. "But sometimes a mother can't keep her baby because she doesn't have a place for him. A baby needs a place that's warm and safe."

"I guess my mother didn't have a good place to keep me," said Michael.

His mom put her arm around him. "I'm sure she would have kept you if she could."

"Does it make a mother sad when she can't keep her baby?"

"I think it must make her very sad," answered his mom. "But it must help her if she knows that someone else will keep her baby safe and well."

A sea gull flapped past Michael's head, crying *K-rrr-ee-ee! K-rrr-ee-ee!* Michael smiled. Maybe that's Henry's sea gull friend. He watched the bird dive into the waves for a fish.

"That old gull was hungry," said his mom.

"Who takes care of a baby when he doesn't have his mother anymore?" Michael asked.

"Sometimes a baby is adopted right away. Or he goes to live in a foster home."

"Like I did."

"Yes."

"I lived in lots of foster homes," said Michael.

"I know," said his mom. "Sometimes babies grow to be big boys and girls before they're adopted."

"Like me," said Michael.

He still wondered about his real mother, and his real father too. Who were they? What happened to them? Maybe someday he'd find out. But for now, things were all right the way they were.

There was only a sprinkling of rain now. Michael and his mom got up and walked along the sand some more, laughing at the sandpipers playing tag with the waves. Michael made footprints on the hard wet sand, and watched as the waves came in and washed them away.

"Did you want to adopt a big boy like me, instead of a baby?" he asked.

"Yes," said his mom. "I wanted to adopt a big boy, just like you."

A bright sliver of light broke through the rain clouds over their heads, outlining the dark clouds with silver. As Michael and his mom looked up, a rainbow arched across the sky.

"This is my favorite Saturday adventure," said Michael.

When they got home, he washed the shells he'd found along the shore and lined them up on the shelf in his room, alongside Henry's little sailing ship. On the wall next to his map of the world, Michael had also put up a picture of a real three-masted ship sailing through a storm.

Now he looked at the ship in the picture, and thought, After the storm is over, I bet there'll be a rainbow. Like today.

Michael looked around his room—it really was *his* room now, full of his special things. Besides his old tow truck and deck of cards, there were all his Hot Wheels tracks and cars, the football he'd gotten for Christmas, the genuine Dallas Cowboys helmet that a friend of his mom's had given him, and his gravestone rubbing of "William S. Riley, A Banjo-Playing Man." And, on his bed, there was the stuffed lion his mom had made him because he was born under the sign of Leo the Lion. . . .

"That's the bravest sign," she'd told him.

Michael sat on his bed, thinking of what his mom had said about wanting to adopt a big boy instead of a baby. I hope she doesn't change her mind! After all, babies are cuter.

He picked up one of the shells, worn smooth and rainbow colored by the sea. *"The biggest thing in the world,"* he whispered.

Then he smiled, as he thought of something else. Babies are cuter, but big boys are better to go on adventures with.

Special Day

The minute he woke up, Michael remembered today was his birthday. He was eight. That's funny, he thought, I don't feel any different.

I wonder what mom's bought me for my birthday? What will we do to celebrate—have a party? Go on a Saturday adventure—even if it isn't Saturday?

As he scrambled out of bed, he smelled bacon cooking. Motorboat meowed at him to hurry up. She smelled the bacon, too.

His mom smiled as he came into the kitchen in his bare feet and pajamas. "Happy birthday," she said, pouring pancake batter on the sizzling griddle.

Bacon and pancakes—his favorite breakfast. Maybe that was his birthday present. It looked good. He was hungry. But he'd still rather have a regular present wrapped up in paper and ribbon, to open as a surprise.

His mom ought to know that!

There was a big slice of honeydew melon beside his

plate, too. His three favorite things for breakfast. He ate a spoonful of juicy melon while his mom heaped pancakes and bacon on his plate.

She smiled. "Hope I made enough for a hungry birthday boy."

Michael didn't feel like smiling back. If everything didn't look so good, he wouldn't even be eating it. Breakfast shouldn't count as a birthday present.

Just as he finished his last pancake, the doorbell jingled. Maybe it was the delivery man with a surprise package, after all. Michael jumped up from the table to see.

When he opened the door it was Lisa and Scott, two new friends from the Christmas party. Michael liked them. They were sort of grown-up, but not quite. Lisa was tall and pretty, with long shining brown hair, and Scott looked and sounded like a cowboy from Texas.

Today they were both wearing jeans, and Scott was carrying a big bag marked fertilizer. He grinned at Michael. "You're going to think it's funny, but this is your birthday present."

A bag of fertilizer? Michael didn't think it was funny at all.

Lisa laughed. Michael guessed *she* thought it was

73

funny. "The fertilizer's only part of your present," she said.

"We're going to plant a birthday garden for you," Scott explained. "Want to go climb into your jeans and give us a hand?"

Plant a garden? That didn't sound like fun. It sounded like work. Some birthday! Michael thought grimly as he put on his jeans.

"Where do you want your garden?" asked Scott, when Michael joined them in the yard.

Michael didn't answer. He didn't want it *anyplace.*

"How about right under your window?" said his mom. "You can look out and watch your garden grow."

He bet this whole idea was his mom's. Other mothers would have thought of a birthday *party* and birthday *presents.* Whoever heard of a birthday *garden?* Why did his mom have to be different all the time!

"Well, let's get to work," said Scott, handing Michael a shovel. "We have to get the ground ready."

While he and Scott broke up the ground with their shovels, his mom and Lisa got down on their knees to pull up the weeds. "You'll have to keep these old weeds out," Lisa reminded Michael.

Great! He was going to have to work *forever* on this dumb garden.

Tony and Peter came down the street. I bet they're going to the playground for a game, thought Michael, and I can't go. I have to stay here and shovel dirt! He jabbed his shovel angrily at the ground.

"What's up?" Tony asked as he and Peter came into the yard.

"We're making a garden," answered Michael. I'm not going to tell them it's for my *birthday*, he thought.

"You guys want to pitch in?" Scott asked them. "The more hands, the better."

"Okay," agreed Tony and Peter, picking up a rake and a hoe and going right to work. Michael was surprised. Who'd want to dig a garden instead of playing ball, if he didn't have to?

Finally, when they got the ground ready, Lisa brought a handful of small envelopes from her purse. There were bright-colored pictures of vegetables on them—carrots and beans, lettuce and tomatoes, cucumbers and corn. "Here's more of your birthday present," she told Michael.

"You mean this garden is your birthday present?"

asked Tony. Peter made a face. "You're going to grow a bunch of old vegetables for your birthday?"

"Sure," said Scott. "Whenever you guys want a snack before a game, you'll be able to pull a carrot right out of the ground."

"Hey—that'll be neat," said Tony.

"It'd be better if it was a Tootsie Roll," said Peter.

"Sorry about that," said Lisa, as she showed Michael how to poke a hole in the ground with his finger, put a few seeds into the hole, then cover it firmly.

The boys helped Michael make careful rows of holes up and down his garden, planting a few seeds in each hole. Then Scott showed them how to fasten the empty seed envelopes onto sticks to make a sign beside each row so Michael would remember what was planted there.

When they were finished, Michael got the hose and gave his garden a sprinkling to get it started. The neatly raked black earth, with the bright little pictures marking each tidy row, made him feel better.

"A garden is a pretty good birthday present," he decided out loud.

"We have three more presents for you," said Scott. "But you have to work for them, too."

"Where are they?" asked Michael. The work was fun, with Tony and Peter helping.

But when he saw his other presents, he was disappointed again. They were just three bare twigs. Lisa smiled. "You'll be surprised how fast they'll grow into trees."

"Real trees?"

"Fruit trees," said Scott. "Every year they'll give you oranges and peaches and plums for your birthday."

"That's better than carrots," said Tony.

"It's still not as good as Tootsie Rolls," said Peter.

The three boys set to work. They dug three deep holes and put water and fertilizer in them. Then Michael held each of the baby trees in place while Tony and Peter packed the dirt around it.

"Now," said Lisa, "let's give your trees and garden a special blessing." She and Scott got their guitars out of the car. Everybody sat in a circle on the grass as Scott started the song:

"Thus the farmer sows his seeds,
Stands erect and takes his ease,
He stamps his foot and claps his hands,
And turns around to view his lands. . . ."

And they all joined in the chorus,

"Oats, peas, beans, and barley grows,
Oats, peas, beans, and barley grows,
Nor you nor I nor anyone knows
How oats, peas, beans, and barley grows. . . ."

They sang some more of Michael's favorite songs. And of course, they also sang,

"Happy birthday, dear Michael,
Happy birthday to you!"

"Close your eyes," said his mom when the song was over. Michael closed his eyes. He felt something in his lap. He touched the crisp folds of paper, the curls of ribbon. A real birthday present!

He opened his eyes and tore off the paper and ribbon.

"Wow! A baseball glove!"

"All *right!*" cheered Tony.

"I'll go get my ball and bat and we'll have some practice," said Peter.

Michael put on his new baseball glove and gave his mom a big hug. How had she known it was just what he wanted? Maybe she wasn't so different from other mothers, after all.

That night, with Motorboat curled up in bed beside him—and his garden growing outside his window—Michael remembered other birthdays that hadn't been as happy as this one. "That house where the people changed their minds and didn't want me—that was the worst," he told Motorboat.

"Meow," Motorboat answered, letting him know she understood.

Then Michael thought about his last birthday, and the party at the County Bureau of Adoptions with the other foster kids. "I blew out all the candles on my cake," he told Motorboat. "And I remembered to make my wish."

Now, his wish had come true—almost. Almost a whole year had gone by since he'd come to live with his new mom. It was the longest time he'd ever stayed in one place. Sometimes he even forgot he wasn't adopted yet. His mom seemed almost like his real mother.

He was sure now that she wouldn't change her mind about adopting him. At least, he didn't *think* so. If only Miss Finch would come and tell him he was finally adopted.

He reached under his bed. His suitcase was still there. But soon he could put it away, up on the shelf in his closet. And forget about it. *Maybe.*

Michael snuggled down in his bed next to Motorboat's warm furry body, closed his eyes tight, and made his birthday wish again.

A Visit to Court

Every day Michael waited for Miss Finch to come and tell him he was adopted. At last, one day when he came home from school, there was her car parked in front of the house.

Michael raced up the front walk and hurried inside. Miss Finch and his mom were in the living room, sitting on the couch with a piece of paper spread out in front of them on the coffee table.

"It's your final adoption paper, Michael," said Miss Finch.

His mom wrote her name at the bottom of the paper, and smiled at Michael. "And now it's all signed and everything."

"Does that mean I'm adopted?" Michael waited quietly for the answer.

"Almost," said Miss Finch.

Almost? He had to blink back *sad* tears this time.

He'd been *almost* adopted a whole year. Wasn't he ever going to be *really* adopted?

"I'm sorry, Michael—but the adoption has to be approved by the court," Miss Finch explained. "You have to go downtown to the courthouse and talk to the judge."

The judge! Michael remembered a judge he had seen on TV. He was a big man wearing a long black robe and sitting up behind a high desk. That judge was mean. He sent people to jail.

I bet the judge won't let me be adopted.

When she got up to leave, Miss Finch gave Michael a hug. Michael was surprised. Miss Finch had never done *that* before.

"Good-bye, Michael dear," she said.

He looked up into her round, kind face and hugged her back. Miss Finch had been like his fairy godmother, who always hurried in when he needed her. But if he was finally going to be adopted, he guessed he wouldn't need a fairy godmother anymore.

If he *didn't* get adopted . . . But he didn't want to think about that.

He watched out the window as Miss Finch hurried

down the walk and drove away in the yellow beetle. He was sure there were lots of other foster children who weren't even *almost* adopted yet, who needed Miss Finch to be their fairy godmother.

Now Michael waited for his mom to say it was time to go downtown to the courthouse. He didn't want to talk to the judge. But he couldn't be adopted until he did.

Finally, a letter came. "We have to go to the courthouse next week," said his mom.

Michael felt scared. I hope the judge isn't too mean.

When it was time, his mom said, "Let's leave the car at home and ride downtown on the bus."

"We never rode on the bus before," said Michael.

"We've never gone to get adopted before," said his mom.

On the bus, Michael dropped their money into the little glass box and took the tickets from the driver. He held on to the chrome bars to keep from falling as they walked down the aisle to a seat.

Michael liked the smell inside the bus, and the *whoosh*ing sound of the doors opening and closing. He watched the people get on and off, and looked out the window as the bus rolled past streets of small wooden houses (that reminded Michael of his street, and his house), along a block of factory buildings, and by a bakery that smelled as good as the homemade bread Henry had made him one day.

The bus turned onto a street of odd-shaped buildings, painted bright reds and greens with gold trimming, and signs in strange black marks Michael couldn't read.

"This is Chinatown," his mom explained.

Michael saw a Chinese boy in a baseball jacket who made him think of Benny, and an old woman wearing a long dress and sandals like Benny's grandmother sometimes wore.

"Better pull the cord," said his mom. "We have to get off at the next stop."

Michael's stomach felt jumpy when he remembered where he was going. He reached up and pulled the cord, the way he had seen the other people do. The bus stopped, and the door *whoosh*ed open to let them off.

Michael looked up at the tall building on the busy downtown street corner. "That's the courthouse," said his mom. Michael's stomach jumped again. His mom took his hand and smiled. "Don't worry—it'll be all right."

They went inside the building and rode the elevator up to a room filled with people. Some were holding babies. Others had boys or girls with them who looked about Michael's age. "They're waiting to be adopted, too," his mom said.

"I've waited a long time to be adopted," said Michael.

"I don't think you'll have to wait much longer," said his mom.

They sat down on a bench next to a large black lady with a little girl beside her. The little girl looked as scared as Michael felt.

A serious-faced man, wearing a uniform like a policeman, called out a name. "Becky Lou Saunders." A couple with a baby got up and followed him into another room.

"He's taking them in to see the judge," explained Michael's mom. Michael thought about it. Maybe a judge who gets babies adopted is different from a judge who sends people to jail.

He listened each time the man in uniform called out

another name. "Jimmy Townsend." A little boy about three years old jumped up. "That's me!" His new parents smiled as they took him by the hand and went in to see the judge.

"Susan Shaw." The scared-looking girl beside Michael got up next.

"Ricky Conover."

"Betty Mills."

As Michael watched the others go in to be adopted, he remembered the roomful of foster kids making their birthday wishes. Maybe everybody's wish could come true, after all.

Did he really want his wish to come true? Did he want to live in his new house with his new mother *forever*?

He'd never ride in the yellow beetle with Miss Finch anymore, and stop at Jack in the Box for hamburgers and Cokes . . .

Or play Bingo with other foster kids around a big dining-room table, munching spicy gingerbread cookies their foster mother had baked for them . . .

Or fall asleep giggling in the dark with other boys, and wake up in the morning to a big pillow fight . . .

"Michael Graham." The man in uniform called his name. Michael scrunched down in his seat. Maybe it would be better if he *didn't* get adopted. . . .

No! He didn't want to go back to a foster home. He liked living with his new mom. And Motorboat and Charlie. He liked his new school, and all his new friends.

"C'mon, honey—it's our turn," said his mom. And he liked the way his mom sometimes called him "honey."

Michael stood up and took her hand. The man in uniform led them to the door of the judge's room. I just hope getting adopted isn't going to change anything, thought Michael, as he followed his mom inside.

Everything in the room was brown—the furniture, the rug, the walls—everything except the judge, who had bright white hair and was wearing his long black robe.

But he wasn't sitting up behind a high desk. He was sitting at a table. And he didn't look mean. He had a friendly face, and he was even smiling.

"Hello, Michael," he said.

"H'lo."

"Would you come and sit down for a minute?" He

motioned Michael and his mom into the two chairs across from him. "I just want to ask you a question or two, all right?"

"Yes, sir."

"How do you feel about your new home?"

"I like it," said Michael.

"And your new mother—would you like to stay with her?"

Michael looked over at his mom with a shy smile. "Yes." He meant to say it in a loud voice, but it came out a whisper. The judge turned away, frowning over a paper on his desk.

Maybe he didn't hear me, worried Michael.

Then the judge looked up, smiling again. "The adoption is approved," he said, reaching over to shake Michael's hand.

His mom held out her arms, and Michael snuggled into them.

"Now we can start planning our trip," his mom said when they were back outside waiting for the bus to take them home.

"Our trip?" echoed Michael.

"One day soon we'll get in the car and go on our

biggest Saturday adventure of all. All the way across the country to meet your grandpa."

Michael thought about his suitcase under his bed. He was going to have to pack it again. But this time, it would be different.

"After we go see my grandpa, will we come back home again?" he asked. Michael thought about everything that "home" meant to him now—his cat and his fish, his birthday garden and fruit trees, his room with all his favorite things . . .

His mom smiled. "Yes," she said. "We'll come right back home."